THE Monster and the Tailor

A Ghost Story

Retold and Illustrated by

PAUL GALDONE

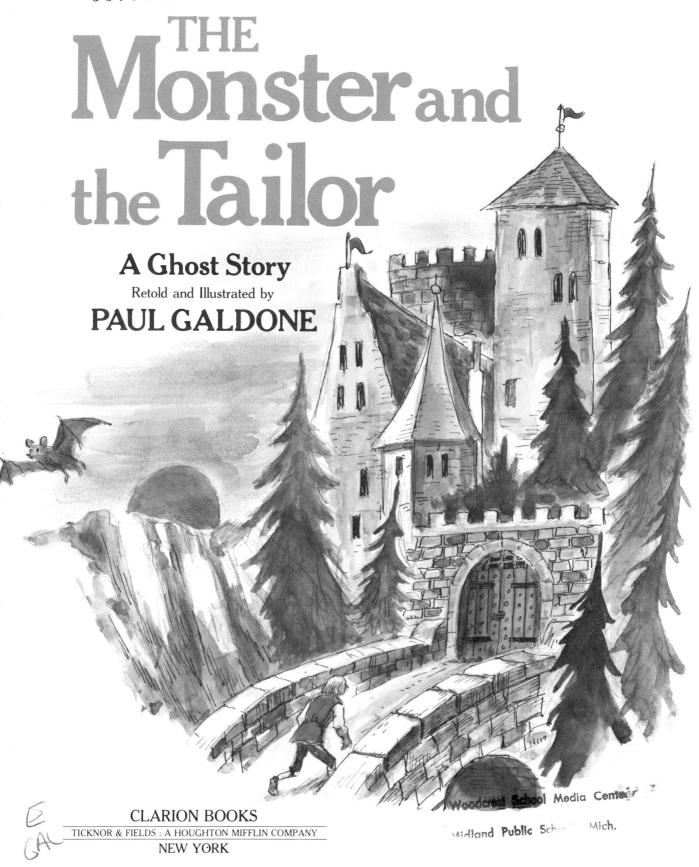

CLARION BOOKS

TICKNOR & FIELDS : A HOUGHTON MIFFLIN COMPANY

NEW YORK

For Adam, Danielle, and Jacqueline

Library of Congress Cataloging in Publication Data

Galdone, Paul.   The monster and the tailor.
Summary: Once there, the tailor quickly regrets his decision to spend
the night in the graveyard sewing lucky trousers for the Duke.
[1. Clothing and dress—Fiction]   I. Title.   PZ7.G1305Mo   [E]
82-1246   ISBN 0-89919-116-9   AACR2

One

day long, long ago, a poor tailor
was summoned to the Grand Duke's castle.

"His Highness wishes to speak with you before
nightfall," the messenger said.

So at twilight the tailor scrambled up the road
to the castle.

"I need a new pair of trousers," the Grand Duke said. "Cut them from this piece of cloth, and make sure that they are handsome and comfortable."

"Your wish is my command, your Highness," the tailor answered.

The Grand Duke nodded. "Now listen carefully," he said. "You must stitch the trousers in the old graveyard at night. Only then will I have good luck when I wear them—that is what my soothsayer told me."

Now everyone knew that the old graveyard was haunted and that weird things went on there after dark. But no one ever refused a command from the Grand Duke.

"I will not be afraid to stitch the trousers in the graveyard," the tailor said boldly.

"Good," said the Grand Duke. "And when you return, a purse full of gold will be yours!"

The tailor hurried back to his shop
to get his sewing things and a candle.
He was afraid, but still he set off
into the night.

As he tramped up the valley, the night grew darker and darker. Finally he reached the eerie old graveyard.

The tailor chose a nice gravestone for a seat, lit
his candle, and began to sew the trousers. In and
out of the cloth his needle flew.

"Why, this graveyard isn't haunted at all," the
tailor reassured himself. "Soon I will be finished
with my task."

He had barely said the last word when the ground
around him began to tremble.

Suddenly the tailor saw a huge head coming up through the ground.

But he kept on stitching.

When the head was above the gravestones, the monster called out in a horrible voice,

"Do you see this great head of mine?"

The tailor shook all over. "I see that,
but I'll sew this," he replied.
    And he stitched away at the trousers.

The head rose up higher until its neck appeared.
The monster called out,

"Do you see this great neck of mine?"

The tailor felt his heart thump. "I see that, but I'll sew this," he replied.

And he stitched away at the trousers.

The head and the neck kept rising until the monster
towered above the tailor. Again, the monster called out,
"Do you see this great chest of mine?"

The tailor's knees began to knock together. "I see that, but I'll sew this," he replied.

And he stitched away at the trousers.

Still the monster rose up and up and up until
it shook a huge pair of arms at the tailor.
"Do you see these great long arms of mine?"

The tailor's hands were sweaty and cold. "I see those, but I'll sew this," he replied.

And he began to make lightning-fast stitches because he knew he had no time to lose.

The monster grew taller and pulled out one great leg. It stamped that leg on the ground and called out, **"Do you see this great leg of mine?"**

"Oh, yes! I see that, but I'll sew this!"
The tailor's fingers flew so fast that he finished
stitching the trousers just as the monster pulled out its other leg.

Quickly the tailor gathered up the trousers, blew
out the candle, jumped from the stone, and ran out of
the graveyard.

"STOP!" the monster roared. It stamped both feet
so hard that the old churchbell rang.

Then it began chasing after the tailor.

Down the valley the tailor ran. Behind him, the monster took great long strides and was soon very close.

"No one gets away from me," the monster cried. "STOP AT ONCE!"

"I will never stop!" the tailor shouted.
He held on tightly to the trousers, and at last
he reached the Grand Duke's castle.

"Open up!" the tailor yelled, as he pounded
on the big wooden gate. "Open up and let me in!"
The tailor looked back and saw the monster
reaching out a great hand to snatch him away.
Just then, the gate opened a crack and
the tailor darted inside.

That is how the Grand Duke got his lucky trousers.

And that is how the poor tailor got his purse full of gold.

As for the monster . . .

. . . he was never seen again after that night.

But the mark of his five great fingers can still be found on the castle wall.

DATE		
~~VIDEO~~ A = EaTT		
C-19		
~~E-19~~		
~~E~~		X